06/19

- 6 AUG 2019

- 9 AUG 2019

- 2 SEP 2019

- 3 JAN 2020

0 1 FEB 2020

Southwark Council

KINGSWOOD LIBRARY
Kingswood House, Seeley Drive
London SE21 8QR

www.southwark.gov.uk/libraries   @SouthwarkLibs

Please return/renew this item by
the last date shown.
Books may also be renewed by
phone and Internet.

D0336963

SK 2705030 0

LADYBIRD BOOKS

UK | USA | Canada | Ireland | Australia | India | New Zealand | South Africa

Ladybird Books is part of the Penguin Random House group of companies whose addresses can be found at global.penguinrandomhouse.com.

www.penguin.co.uk   www.puffin.co.uk   www.ladybird.co.uk

Penguin
Random House
UK

First published 2019
001

Adapted by Lauren Holowaty

This book copyright © Astley Baker Davies Ltd/Entertainment One UK Ltd 2019

This book is based on the TV series Peppa Pig.
Peppa Pig is created by Neville Astley and Mark Baker.
Peppa Pig © Astley Baker Davies Ltd/Entertainment One UK Ltd 2003.
www.peppapig.com

Printed in China

A CIP catalogue record for this book is available from the British Library

ISBN: 978-0-241-37165-7

All correspondence to:
Ladybird Books
Penguin Random House Children's
80 Strand, London WC2R 0RL

MIX
Paper from
responsible sources
FSC
www.fsc.org   FSC® C018179

It was Space Day at playgroup.
Peppa and her friends were very excited.
"Does anyone know what space is?" asked Madame Gazelle.
"Space is the physical universe beyond the Earth's atmosphere,"
said Edmond Elephant. Edmond was a bit of a clever clogs.
"That's right, Edmond," said Madame Gazelle. "And today
we are going to talk about something you find in space . . ."

"The moon?" shouted all the children.
"Yes," said Madame Gazelle.

"Can I live on the moon?" asked Danny Dog.
"It is possible," replied Madame Gazelle.
"But you would need to take oxygen, water
and lots of other things with you."

"Can you jump in muddy puddles on the moon?" asked Peppa.
"No," said Madame Gazelle. "There is no rain to make puddles."

"What *can* you do on the moon, then?" asked Peppa.
"You'll soon find out," said Madame Gazelle,
"because **today** we are going to the . . ."

"MOON!" shouted Pedro Pony.
"Not exactly," said Madame Gazelle.
"We're going to the Space Museum."
"Oh," sighed the children.

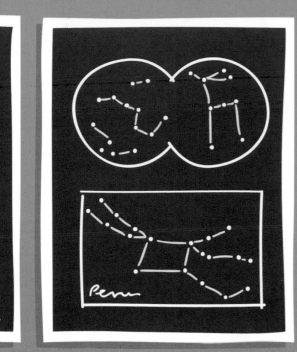

"At the museum you will train to be astronauts," said Madame Gazelle, "and see what it's like to walk on the moon."

"Wow!" gasped the children.

Miss Rabbit arrived to take everyone to the Space Museum.

"Really, we should be going there in a moon buggy," said Danny, "not a bus."

"How long until we get there?" asked Peppa.
"As long as it takes you to finish your apple,"
replied Miss Rabbit.
"I've finished my apple," said Suzy Sheep.
"Does that mean we're there?"

"How about we sing a song for Miss Rabbit?"
suggested Madame Gazelle. "Something like . . ."
But, before Madame Gazelle could finish,
all the children started to sing.

"We're going to the moo-oo-oo-oo-oon . . .
Will we get there soo-oo-oo-oo-oon?"

And they sang it to Miss Rabbit
all the way to the museum!

When they arrived at the museum, the children
were met by a real astronaut . . . Grampy Rabbit!

"Hello there, fellow astronauts," he boomed. "Our space-training mission today will take us to the moon! The ride may be bumpy, but it will be worth it when you get to see what it's like to walk on the moon!"

"Hooray!" cheered the children.

The children put on their special spacesuits
and boots as quickly as they could.
"It's time to hop on board our spacecraft,"
called Grampy Rabbit when they were ready.

"Five, four, three, two, one . . ."

"Blast off!" cheered all the little astronauts together.

Grampy Rabbit and the children zoomed off on their training mission!

On the way to the moon, Grampy Rabbit told the children all about the different planets in the solar system. "There's Mercury, Venus, Earth, Mars, Jupiter, Saturn, Uranus, Neptune and the dwarf planet, Pluto," he said. "Robots have landed on Mars, but no one else has done so . . . yet!"

George was listening very carefully.
"Mars!" he whispered to himself.

BUMP!

"We have landed on the moon," said Grampy Rabbit. "Now, my little astronauts, it's time for you to see what it's like to walk on the moon. Just take one small step out of the spacecraft, and one . . ."

Peppa and her friends all took **giant leaps** out of the spacecraft wearing Grampy Rabbit's anti-gravity rubber bands.

Wheeeeeeeee!

The children had so much fun bouncing up
and down with the anti-gravity rubber bands!
They sang a song over and over again:
"*Listen to our space tu-uu-uu-uu-uuune . . .*
We're walking on the moo-oo-oo-oo-ooon!"

BOING!

BOING!

BOING!

"Wow!" gasped Peppa, bouncing over Madame Gazelle's head. "Walking on the moon is great, but jumping up and down on it is even better!"

"It's time to get back down to Earth now, children," called Grampy Rabbit.

"Ohhh!" sighed the children.

When they arrived back on Earth, the children were sad.
"Remember, children, your adventure isn't really over,"
said Grampy Rabbit. "It's just beginning. If you keep
training, you can all be real astronauts like me one day!"

"**Yay!** *We're going to the moo-oo-oo-oo-ooon!*"
sang the children. And they sang it on the bus
all the way back to playgroup!

"Space is amazing, Daddy!" said Peppa that night.
"I want to be an astronaut so I can jump up
and down on the moon every day!"
But George had set his sights on somewhere else.
"Mars," he whispered.

"Ahh," said Daddy Pig. "Are you going to be the first piggy on Mars, George?" George nodded his head and smiled.

That night, George dreamt he had gone into space with Peppa, and they were the first little piggies ever to jump up and down . . .

. . . on Mars!